Sepren's Christmas Adventure

by
Winnie
Hirsch

Other books in the Sepren Series:

Sepren's Easter Adventure
Sepren's 4th of July Adventure

for a complete listing of books, please
visit www.winniehirsch.com

first edition printed 12/2014

Once upon a time there was a lizard named Sepren. He was not the biggest or most important reptile in his town. But little did he know, soon he would be.

Sepren was walking home one day when he smelled the aroma of fresh baked cricketcakes wafting through the bakery's open window. He was looking longingly in at the cricketcakes, when something in the corner of the window caught his eye.

It was a sign. In big, red, bold letters it read…

"SANTA NEEDS A HELPER:
The one who does the kindest deed
will get to be Santa's helper for
Christmas this year."

As Sepren headed home he
wrapped his new, warm cloak around
his shoulders. He was very glad to
have it.

On his way home he saw Sammie the snake. "Hello, Sammie," Sepren said. "What will your kind deed be?"

"I," replied Sammie, "will do do disshesss for my brothersss. I sssure hope Sssanta will pick me!"

Sepren looked skeptical. "Bye-bye Sammie!" he said.

"Goodbye, Sssepren," replied Sammie. And he went on his way.

Sepren had almost reached home, when he saw a small, cold-looking salamander standing in the snow. It was shivering all over and was obviously freezing.

Without thinking, Sepren took off his cloak and wrapped it around the little salamander. Then he smiled and walked the rest of the way home, shivering.

All too quickly, Christmas Eve came, the night when Santa was to choose his helper.

Sepren was sad that he hadn't found a kind deed to do yet, but he decided to head to the town square anyway, and see who would be picked.

By the time he got there, a huge crowd had already gathered. Just about everyone from the town was there.

Finally a small elf dressed in blue and red clothes came out from the shop.

"Santa has chosen!" The elf announced. "Sepren, you are to be Santa's helper!"

Everyone in the crowd turned to cheer for Sepren. He was surprised, since he hadn't done a good deed.

Then he remembered the little Salamander. He had done a kind deed without even knowing it!

Just then, Sepren felt a tap on his shoulder. "Come with me," said the elf, "we need to prepare Santa's sleigh."

First, they loaded the sleigh with Santa's toy bags. Then they hitched up the reindeer, and they were just in time.

Santa came out in his red suit and in a jolly voice said, "Hello, Sepren! I'm glad you can help me. Thank you very much."

"You're welcome, sir," replied Sepren.

"Now," said Santa, "why don't you hop in the sack so we can be on our way. I wouldn't want you to fall out of the sleigh!"

"Up, up and away!" shouted Santa as they zoomed over the rooftops.

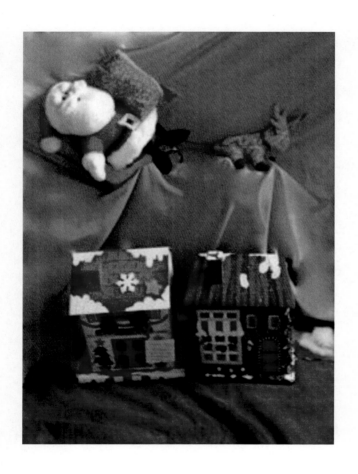

Their first stop was a small neighborhood.

"I'll get these houses, and you get that one," Santa told Sepren, while pointing to a small, red and green house. "Alright," said Sepren excited-ly.

So he started on his task. He quietly crept down the chimney with his bag of toys. Then he tiptoed over to the Christmas tree and gently laid a small red and gold present under it.

Quickly he crept back up the chimney and out to the sleigh to wait for Santa.

After visiting every home in the world, Santa finally dropped Sepren off at his own house.

"Sepren," said Santa, "you really helped me out tonight, and I would like to thank you."

And with that he handed Sepren a present wrapped in green and gold paper. Sepren unwrapped the package carefully, and found a new, lovely cloak decorated with winter scenes and a silk tie.

He turned to thank Santa, but he had disappeared.

Sepren looked up to the sky and saw the sleigh flying away silhouetted by the moon.

He went inside to make some mealworm eggnog, and rest from his big night.

But while he was sitting and sipping the hot eggnog, there came a pounding on the door...

stay tuned for Sepren's next adventure

About the Author:
Winnie Hirsch is now 12 years old and lives on a farm in Cedaredge, Colorado. She has a pet bearded dragon, Sepren, who is the inspiration for these stories. There is also Millie the sala-mander, along with two sisters, one brother, nine cats, one dog, two guinea pigs, one rabbit, five alpacas, ten cows, nine yaks, 24 chickens, two pigs, and a mother and father who are both veterinarians. Thankfully, only Millie and Sepren share her room. She is home-schooled at the veterinary clinic, and has a very active imagination.

Outtakes:

20729466R00015

Made in the USA
San Bernardino, CA
28 December 2018